W9-BWW-167

THE LOST PACKAGE

RICHARD HO

illustrated by JESSICA LANAN

Roaring Brook Press
New York

Published by Roaring Brook Press
Roaring Brook Press is a division of Holtzbrinck Publishing Holdings Limited Partnership
120 Broadway, New York, NY 10271
mackids.com

Library of Congress Control Number: 2020912150

ISBN 978-1-250-23135-2

Our books may be purchased in bulk for promotional, educational, or business use. Please contact your local bookseller or the Macmillan Corporate and Premium Sales Department at (800) 221-7945 ext. 5442 or by email at MacmillanSpecialMarkets@macmillan.com.

First edition, 2021

Book design by Mercedes Padró
The illustrations for this book were created with watercolors.

Printed in China by RR Donnelley Asia Printing Solutions Ltd., Dongguan City, Guangdong Province

1 3 5 7 9 10 8 6 4 2

Like other packages, this one began as an empty box.

It was packed with great care,

sealed tight,

and given
a personal
touch.

At the post office, it was weighed,   stamped,

labeled,

and loaded onto a truck.

Like other packages, it was taken to a building with wondrous machines.

Machines that zip mail through a maze of moving belts.

Machines that tumble and separate,

scan and measure,

sort and route.

Like other packages, this one headed to the airport.

But before it got there,

Now

it

was

Like other lost packages, this one seemed hidden,

invisible,

and forgotten.

Until . . .

. . . it was **found.**

The package was tattered and muddy,

but its destination was clear.

Like all packages, this one was sent with hope

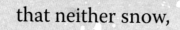

that neither snow,

nor rain,

nor heat,

nor gloom of night

will keep it from being delivered.

Not all packages travel the same road.

Some get lost.

Some get found.

But most end up where
they were meant to be.